D1095508

Manatees

A Level One Reader

By Cynthia Klingel and Robert B. Noyed

The Child's World®

What is big and gray and swims in the water? A manatee!

Manatees can weigh 1,000 pounds (454 kilograms).

They are sometimes called sea cows.

Manatees have dark
gray skin.

They have a flat tail
and two flippers.

They move their tails
up and down to swim.

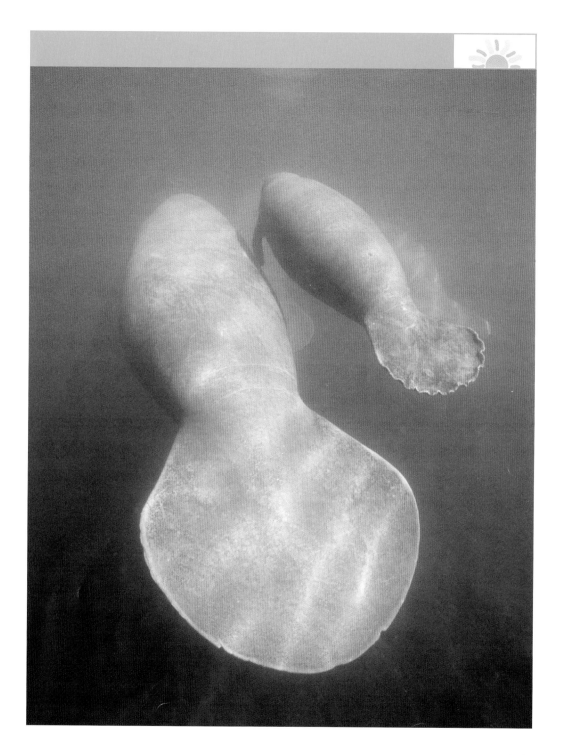

Manatees live where it is warm.

They eat water plants.

Manatees move very slowly in the water.

People enjoy watching manatees swim.

Word List

flat

flippers

kilograms

pounds

tail

Note to Parents and Educators

Welcome to The Wonders of Reading™! These books provide text at three different levels for beginning readers to practice and strengthen their reading skills. In addition, the use of nonfiction text gives readers the valuable opportunity to *read to learn*, not just to learn to read.

These leveled readers allow children to choose books at their level of reading confidence and performance. Level One books offer beginning readers simple language, word choice, and sentence structure as well as a word list. Level Two books feature slightly more difficult vocabulary, longer sentences, and longer total text. In the back of each Level Two book are an index and a list of books and Web sites for finding out more information. Level Three books continue to extend word choice and length of text. In the back of each Level Three book are a glossary, an index, and a list of books and Web sites for further research.

State and national standards in reading and language arts emphasize using nonfiction at all levels of reading development. The Wonders of Reading™ books fill the historical void in nonfiction for primary grade readers with the additional benefit of a leveled text.

About the Authors

Cynthia Klingel has worked as a high school English teacher and an elementary teacher. She is currently the curriculum director for a Minnesota school district. Writing children's books is another way for her to continue her passion for sharing the written word with children. Cynthia is a frequent visitor to the children's section of bookstores and enjoys spending time with her many friends, family, and two daughters.

Robert Noyed started his career as a newspaper reporter. Since then, he has worked in communications and public relations for more than fourteen years for a Minnesota school district. He enjoys writing books for children and finds that it brings a different feeling of challenge and accomplishment from other writing projects. He is an avid reader who also enjoys music, theater, traveling, and spending time with his wife, son, and daughter.

Published by The Child's World®, Inc.
PO Box 326
Chanhassen, MN 55317-0326
800-599-READ
www.childsworld.com

Photo Credits
© 2002 Art Wolfe/Stone: 6
© Jeff Greenberg/Unicorn Stock Photos: 9
© 1993 Mark J. Thomas/Dembinsky Photo Assoc. Inc.: 2, 18
© 2002 Nikolas Konstantinou/Stone: 5
© 2002 D & K Tapparel/Stone: 10
© Sharksong/M. Kazmers/Dembinsky Photo Assoc. Inc.: 13, 17, 21
© 2002 Stuart Westmorland/Stone: cover, 14

Project Coordination: Editorial Directions, Inc.
Photo Research: Alice K. Flanagan

Library of Congress Cataloging-in-Publication Data
Klingel, Cynthia Fitterer.
Manatees / by Cynthia Klingel and Robert B. Noyed.
     p. cm.
ISBN 1-56766-944-1 (lib. bdg. : alk. paper) *25212498 9/01*
1. Manatees—Juvenile literature. [1. Manatees.]
I. Noyed, Robert B. II. Title.
QL737.S63 K65 2001
599.55—dc21
                              00-011366